L•Leonard

ro vocal

BETTER THAN KARAOKE!

'NGBOOK & SOUND-ALIKE CD
TH UNIQUE *PITCH-CHANGER*™

HIGH SCHOOL

GW00888771

CONTENTS

Page	Title	DEMO TRACK	SING-ALONG TRACK
2	CAN I HAVE THIS DANCE	1	9
7	HIGH SCHOOL MUSICAL	2	10
13	I WANT IT ALL	3	11
21	A NIGHT TO REMEMBER	4	12
28	NOW OR NEVER	5	13
34	RIGHT HERE RIGHT NOW	6	14
39	SCREAM	7	15
44	WALK AWAY	8	16

ISBN 978-1-4234-6533-1

Walt Disney Music Company

DISTRIBUTED BY

HAL•LEONARD®
CORPORATION

7777 W. BLUEMOUND RD. P.O. BOX 13819 MILWAUKEE, WI 53213

In Australia Contact:
Hal Leonard Australia Pty. Ltd.
4 Lentara Court
Cheltenham, Victoria, 3192 Australia
Email: ausadmin@halleonard.com.au

Visit Hal Leonard Online at
www.halleonard.com

Can I Have This Dance

**Words and Music by Adam Anders
and Nikki Hassman**

- ing the way _____ we do.

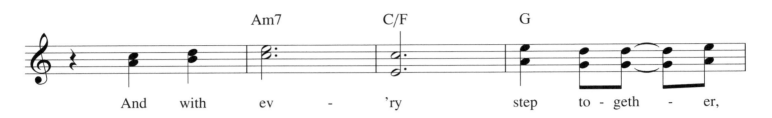

And with ev - 'ry step to - geth - er,

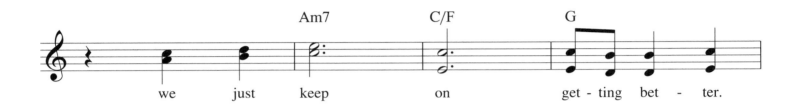

we just keep on get - ting bet - ter.

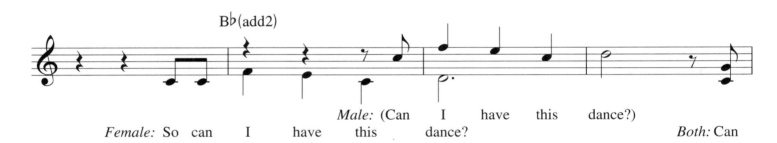

Male: (Can I have this dance?)

Female: So can I have this dance? *Both:* Can

I have this _____ dance? _____ *Female:* Can

Outro

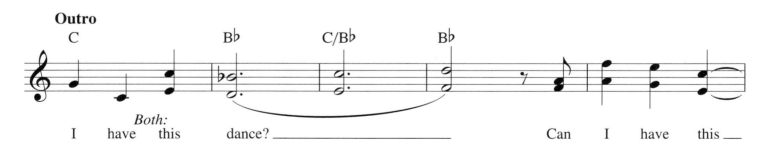

Both:
I have this dance? _____ Can I have this ___

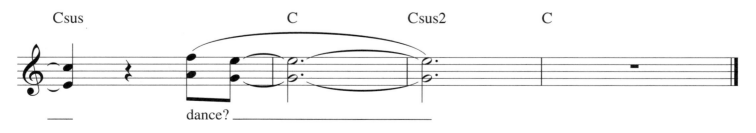

___ dance? _____

High School Musical

**Words and Music by Matthew Gerrard
and Robbie Nevil**

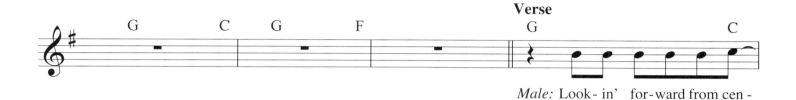

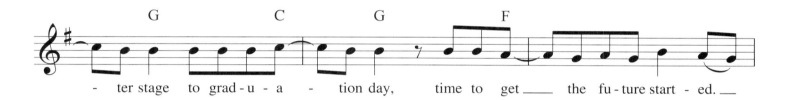

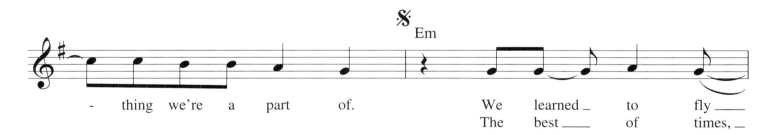

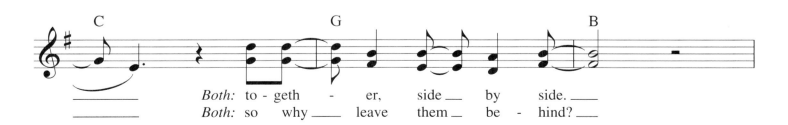

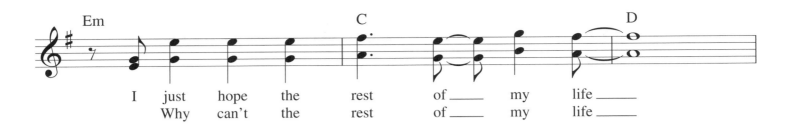

I just hope the rest of ____ my life ____
Why can't the rest of ____ my life ____

Chorus

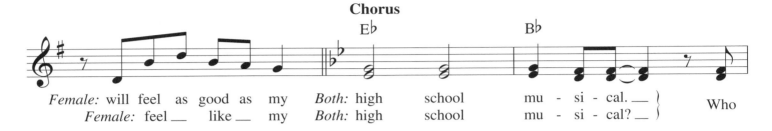

Female: will feel as good as my *Both:* high school mu - si - cal. ____ Who
Female: feel ____ like ____ my *Both:* high school mu - si - cal? ____

says we have to let it go? ____ It's the best part we've ev -

- er known; ____ step in - to the fu - ture, ____ but hold on to

high school mu - si - cal. ____ Let's cel - e - brate ____ where we ____

____ come from, ____ the friends who've been ____ there all ____

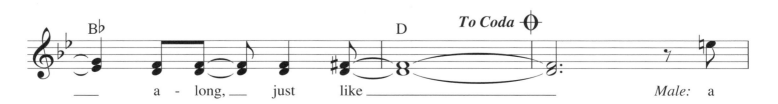

____ a - long, ____ just like _____ *Male:* a

8

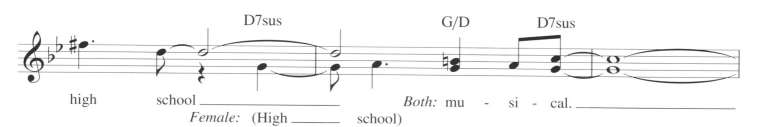

high school _____ *Both:* mu - si - cal. _____

Female: (High _____ school)

Verse

_____ Im - prov - i - sa - tion with - out _____ a script. No one's writ -

- ten it, *Male:* and now _____ we have a chance to. *Female:* But some - day we'll be look-

D.S. al Coda

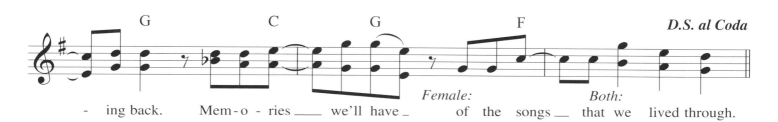

- ing back. Mem - o - ries _____ we'll have _ of the songs __ that we lived through.

Female: *Both:*

Coda   **Bridge**

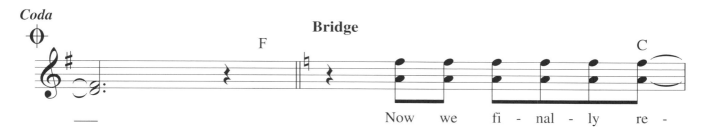

_____ Now we fi - nal - ly re -

- al - ize _____ *Female:* who we are. It just took _____ some time. _

Both: We had to live, and to learn _____ to see _____ the truth, _____

that noth-ing's ev - er im - pos - si - ble. __

In - to the fu - ture we all __ free fall __ and pray for - ev - er we'll al -

- ways have __ high school. _____

Male: Time to par - ty, now cel - e - brate, *Female:* 'cause the

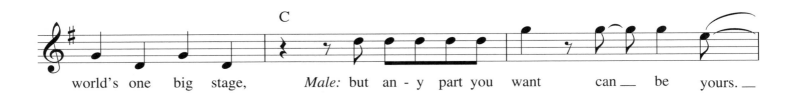

world's one big stage, *Male:* but an - y part you want can __ be yours. __

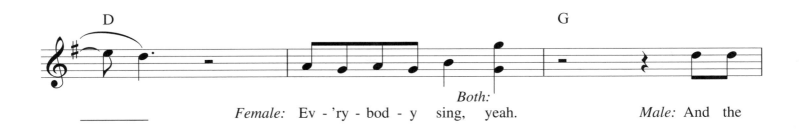

_____ *Female:* Ev - 'ry - bod - y sing, yeah.
Both:
Male: And the

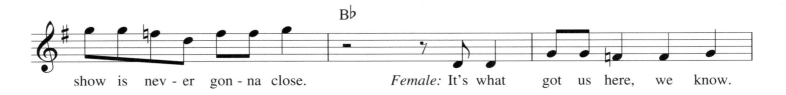

show is nev - er gon - na close. *Female:* It's what got us here, we know.

Both: High school lives on for - ev - er - more. ___

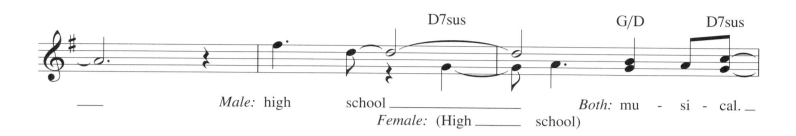

___ Male: high school ___ Both: mu - si - cal. ___

Female: (High ___ school)

Chorus

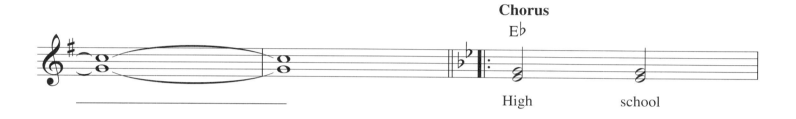

___ High school

mu - si - cal. ___ Who says we have to let it go? ___

It's the best part we've ev - er known; ___ step in - to the fu - ture, ___

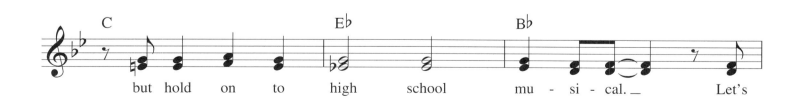

but hold on to high school mu - si - cal. ___ Let's

F   **1** C   E♭

cel - e - brate _ where we _ come from, _ the friends who've been _ there all _

B♭   D

_ a - long, _ oh yeah. _____

2 C   **Outro**   Cm7   B♭/D

_ come from. _ *Female:* All to - geth - er makes it bet - ter.

E♭6   B♭/D   Cm7

Male: Mem - o - ries that last for - ev - er. *Both:* I want the rest of

B♭/D   A♭

my life to feel just _ like _____ a _____

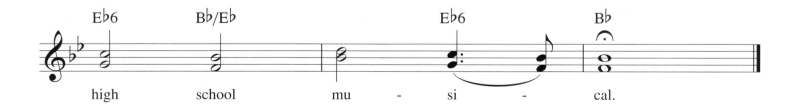

E♭6   B♭/E♭   E♭6   B♭

high school mu - si - cal.

I Want It All

Words and Music by Matthew Gerrard
and Robbie Nevil

Intro
Moderately fast

Verse

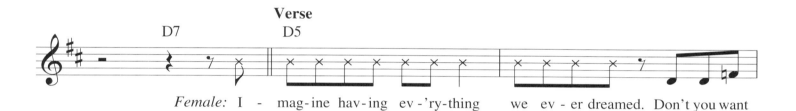

Female: I - mag-ine hav-ing ev -'ry-thing we ev - er dreamed. Don't you want

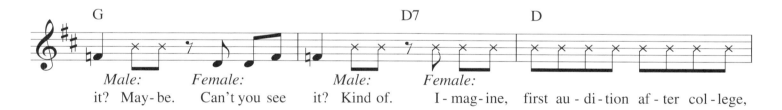

Male: it? May-be. *Female:* Can't you see it? *Male:* Kind of. *Female:* I-mag-ine, first au-di-tion af - ter col-lege,

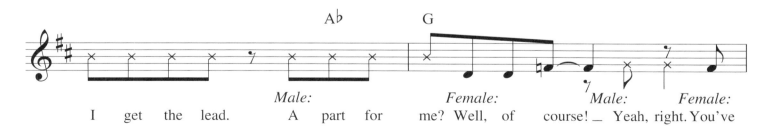

I get the lead. *Male:* A part for me? *Female:* Well, of course! _ *Male:* Yeah, right. *Female:* You've

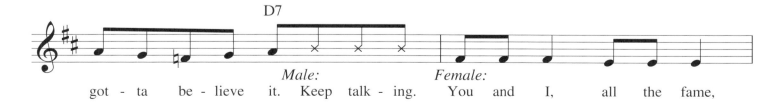

Male: got - ta be - lieve it. Keep talk-ing. *Female:* You and I, all the fame,

Male:
Shar - pay and "What's - his - name."

Female:
Sound ex - cit - ing?

Male:
In - vit - ing.

Female:
Let's do it, then.

Male:
I'm lis - ten - ing.

Female:
Per - son - al sty - l - ist,

a - gent and a pub - li - cist.

Male:
But where do I fit in - to this?

Female:
With you, we can win.

Male:
Win the part? ___

Female:
Think big - ger.

Male:
Be - come su - per - stars? ___

Female:
___ That's bet - ter. Don't you see that big - ger is bet - ter, and bet - ter is big - ger? A lit - tle bit is nev - er e - nough, no, no, no. Don't you want it all?

Chorus

Both:
You want ___ it, you know ___ that you want ___ it,
I want ___ it, ___ want ___ it, ___ want ___

the fame ___ and the for - tune, and more. ___

Female:
You want it
I want it

CODA

D

Both:
all, I want it, want it, want it, Ra - di -

C   **G**   **A**

o Cit - y Mu - sic Hall. We want it

Bridge

B   **F♯7sus**   **B**

all. *Male:* Here in the spot - light we shine; look at who we are.

F♯7sus   **C**   **G7sus**

Female: When Broad - way knows your name, *Both:* you

C   **D♭7sus**   **E♭7sus**

know that you're a star.

Interlude 1
Double-time Swing (♩♩ = ♩ ♪)

F♯7sus   **C/D**   **E♭/F**

(1.) Dance!

N.C.   **C/D** **E♭/F** **D♭7sus**

(Spoken): Madison Square Garden!
(2.) ...again.   *She wants you on the show.*   *They're gonna have to get back to you.*

I, I want it, want it. I want it, I, I, I want it all.
I'd love to, I'd love to, I have to, I want to, I want it.

Backing vocals:
Big-ger is bet-ter, and bet-ter is big-ger, and big-ger is bet-ter and

I want it, I, I, I want it, want it. I want it, I,
I want it. I have to have it, oh, I want it. I have to...

Chorus

bet-ter is big-ger.

Female:
I, I, I want it all! _____
Both: I want it, want it, want it,

the fame and the for - tune, and more. I want it all. I want it, want

Female: *Both:*

Swing (♩♩ = ♩♪)

it, want it. I've got-ta have my star on the door. I want the

Female:

world, noth-ing less, all the glam and the press on - ly giv-ing me the best re - views.

20

A Night to Remember

**Words and Music by Matthew Gerrard
and Robbie Nevil**

Intro
Moderately fast

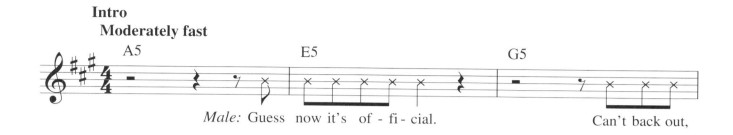

Male: Guess now it's of-fi-cial. Can't back out,

can't back out, no! Get-tin' read-y for the night of nights, the

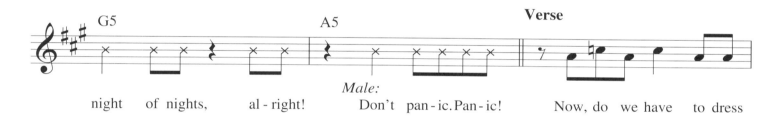

night of nights, al-right! *Male:* Don't pan-ic. Pan-ic! Now, do we have to dress

Verse

up for the prom?__ Dude, I don't think we have the choice.__ *Female:* Yeah, it's the

night of all nights, got-ta look just right,_ dress-in' to im-press the boys._

__ *Male:* Do I want clas-sic or vin-tage or plaid?

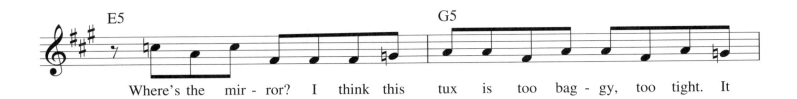

Where's the mir - ror? I think this tux is too bag - gy, too tight. It

Female:
makes me look weird. Should I go mo - vie - star glam - or - ous,

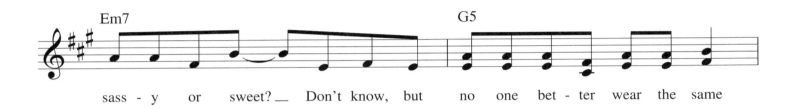

sass - y or sweet? __ Don't know, but no one bet - ter wear the same

Male: *Female:* It's the night __
dress __ as me. __ It's the night _____ of our night - mares.

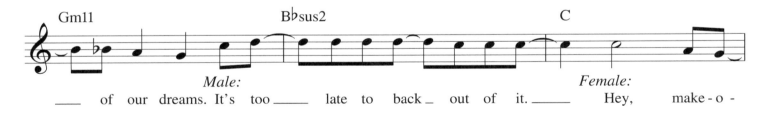

Male: *Female:*
__ of our dreams. It's too __ late to back _ out of it. _____ Hey, make - o -

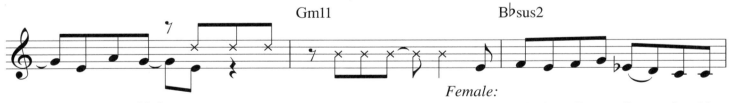

Female:
Male: Don't know what a cor - sage _ is. Been wait - in' all our lives _ for this.
- vers, mas - sag - es.

Chorus

Male: *Female:*
It's gon - na be a night _____ (Can't wait.) to re - mem -

Bb   C5

Male: *Female:*

- ber. (Oh, man.) Come on now.   Big fun.   Al-right!   It's gon-na be   the night __

Ab   Bb   Cm

Male: *Female:*   *Male:*   *Both:*

__   (I guess.) to last for-ev - er, (Luck-y us.) we'll nev-er, ev-er, ev-er for-get. __

Verse

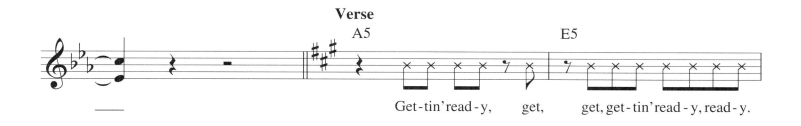

A5   E5

__   Get-tin' read-y,   get,   get, get-tin' read-y, read-y.

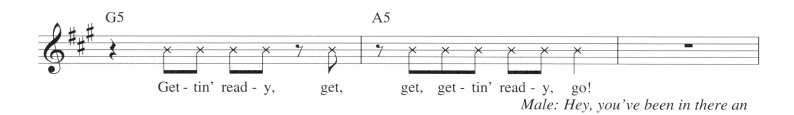

G5   A5

Get-tin' read-y,   get,   get, get-tin' read-y,   go!

Male: Hey, you've been in there an

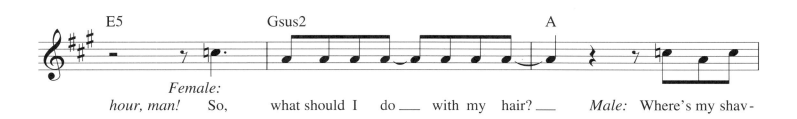

E5   Gsus2   A

Female:

hour, man! So,   what should I   do __ with my hair? __   *Male:* Where's my shav-

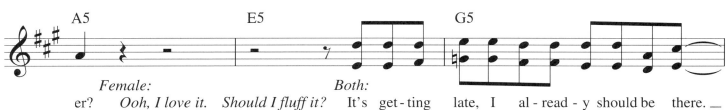

A5   E5   G5

Female: *Both:*

er?   *Ooh, I love it. Should I fluff it?* It's get-ting   late, I   al-read-y should be   there. __

     Male: I look like a waiter.

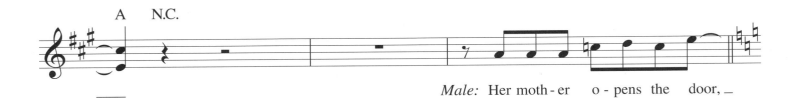

A   N.C.

_____

Male: Her moth - er o - pens the door, _____

C   Gm11   B♭sus2

_____ I'm shak-ing in - side. _____ *Female:* He's here, _____ it's time, _ the hour's _____

C

_____ ar - rived. _ Don't know why _____ her fa - ther's star - ing me down. _____

Gm11   B♭sus2

_____ *Female:* Where's my purse, lip gloss? Now I'm real -

C

ly freak - ing out. _____ *Male:* Then some - thing chang - es my world, _

Gm11   B♭sus2

_____ the most beau - ti - ful girl, _____ right in front of my eyes. _

Both:
prob-ab - ly should. _ Big fun! Male: On the night of nights, (Al - right.) the

N.C.

Female: Male:

night of nights, to-night. Both: Let's dance on the

night of nights. You know we're gon - na do it right. It's gon-na be the night _

Chorus

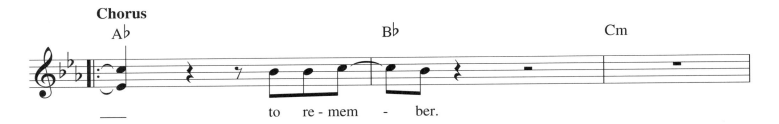

Ab   Bb   Cm

_ to re - mem - ber.

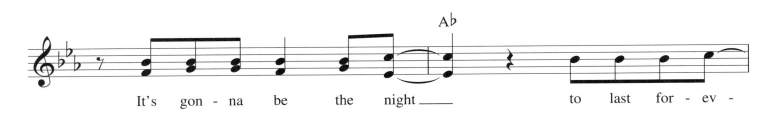

It's gon - na be the night _____ to last for - ev -

Ab

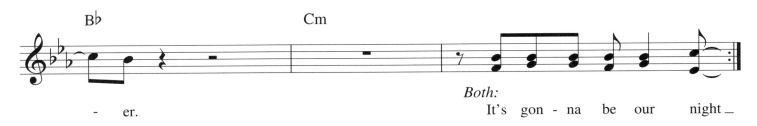

Bb   Cm

- er.   Both: It's gon - na be our night _

Chorus-Outro

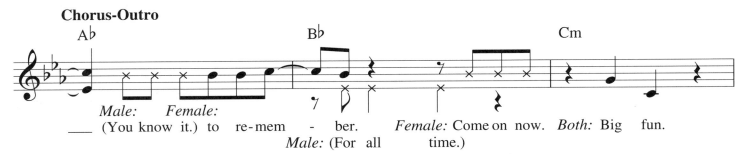

Ab   Bb   Cm

Male: Female:
_ (You know it.) to re - mem - ber. Female: Come on now. Both: Big fun.
Male: (For all time.)

26

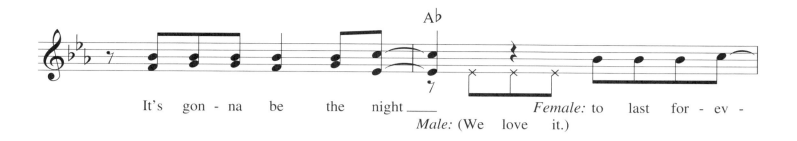

It's gon - na be the night _____   *Female:* to last for - ev -
Male: (We love it.)

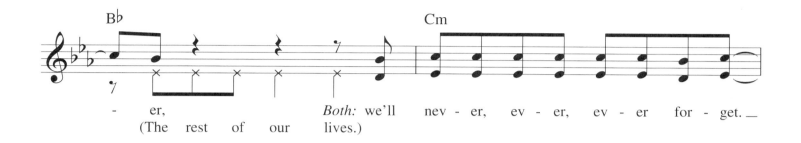

\- er,   *Both:* we'll nev - er, ev - er, ev - er for - get. ___
(The rest of our lives.)

_____ It's gon - na be our night. ____   *Male:*   *Female:*
(Oh, yeah.) ____ All to - geth -

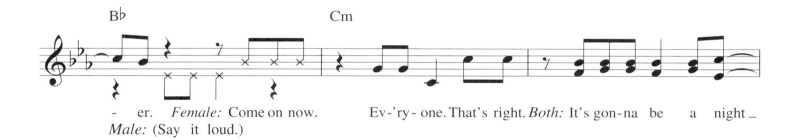

\- er. *Female:* Come on now.   Ev - 'ry - one. That's right. *Both:* It's gon-na be a night ___
Male: (Say it loud.)

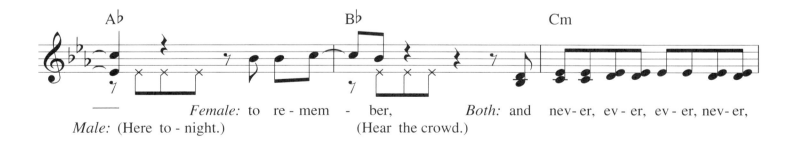

_____   *Female:* to re - mem - ber,   *Both:* and nev - er, ev - er, ev - er, nev - er,
Male: (Here to - night.)   (Hear the crowd.)

ev - er, ev - er, nev - er, ev - er,   nev - er, ev - er, ev - er for - get. ___

Now or Never

Words and Music by Matthew Gerrard
and Robbie Nevil

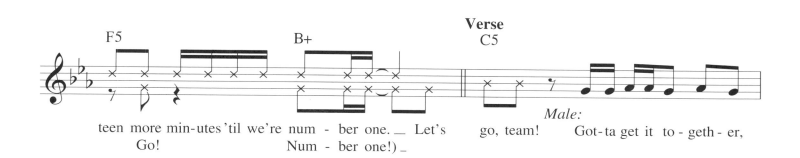

Verse

teen more min-utes 'til we're num - ber one. __ Let's   go, team!   Got-ta get it to - geth - er,
Go!   Num - ber one!) _

Male:

yeah, pull up and shoot! (Score!)   Are you read - y, are you with   me?

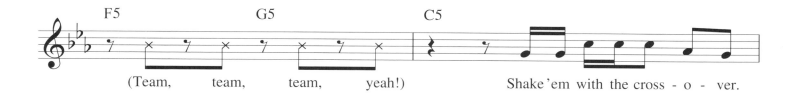

(Team,   team,   team,   yeah!)   Shake 'em with the cross - o - ver.

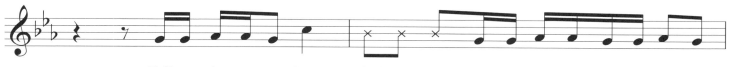

Tell me, what are we   here   for? (To win!) 'Cause we know that we're the best team.

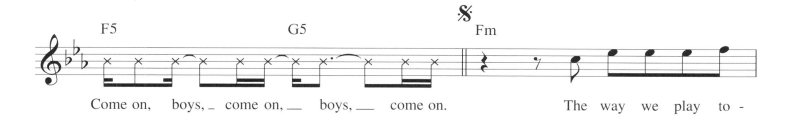

Come on,   boys, _ come on, __ boys, ___ come on.   The   way   we   play   to -

night   is what we leave be - hind. _   It   all comes down to   right   now. It's up   to us. __

____   So what are we gon - na   be?   (T - E - A - M, team!)   Got-ta work it

29

Chorus

Bb   B+   Cm

out, turn it on. Come on! This is the last __ time to get it right.

Cm/Bb   Am7b5

This is the last __ chance to make it our night. We got-ta show __ what we're all a - bout,

Ab   Bb(add4)   Cm

work __ to - geth - er. This is the last __ chance to make our mark.

Cm/Bb   Am7b5

His - to - ry ___ will know who we are. This is the last __ game, so make it count; it's

To Coda ⊕ **Interlude 1**

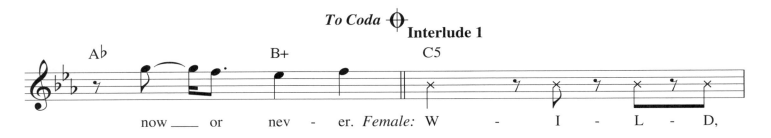

Ab   B+   C5

now ___ or nev - er. *Female:* W - I - L - D,

Wild - cats, you know __ you're on! W - I - L - D,

Wild - cats, come on, __ come on! West High Knights, hey, yeah, we're

do - in' it right, oh yeah! W - I - L - D,

Verse

C5

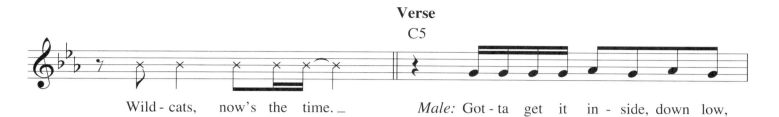

Wild - cats, now's the time. _ *Male:* Got - ta get it in - side, down low,

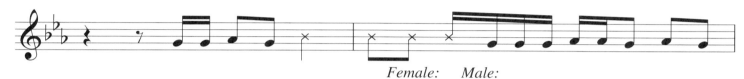

in the paint. Now shoot! *Female:* *Male:* Score! (De - fense!) We got - ta work it to - geth - er.

F5   G5   C5

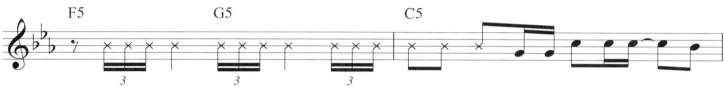

3   3   3

(Gim - me the ball, gim - me the ball, gim - me the ball.) Fast break. Keep the ball in con - trol.

Female: *Female:* (No

Let it fly from down - town. (Three more!) *Troy:* Show 'em we can do it bet - ter

F5   G5   ***D.S. al Coda***   *CODA*   N.C.

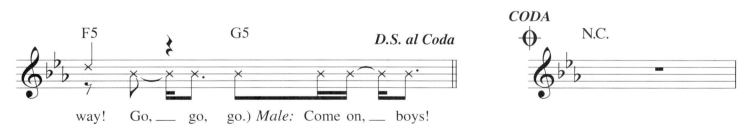

way! Go, _ go, go.) *Male:* Come on, _ boys!

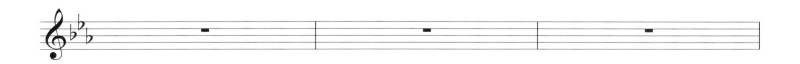

Yeah!   Hey.   We're the   best.   Gon-na win.

Male: Got-ta show 'em how we do it. (Game *Both:* on!)

Chorus

Cm   Cm/B♭

Male: This is the last ___ time to get it right.   This is the last ___ chance to make it our night.

Am7♭5   A♭   B♭(add4)

We got-ta show ___ what we're all a - bout,   work ___ to - geth - er.

Cm   Cm/B♭

This is the last ___ chance to make our mark.   His - to - ry ___ will know who we are.

Am7♭5   **1**   A♭   B+

This is the last ___ game, so make it count; it's   now ___ or nev - er.

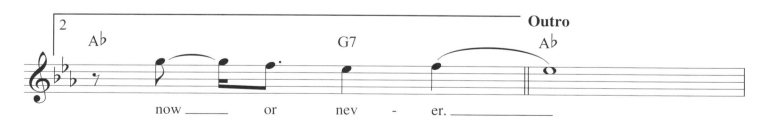

2   A♭   G7   **Outro** A♭

now _____ or nev - er. _____

B♭   Cm

Yeah.

Right Here Right Now

Words and Music by
Jamie Houston

Gmaj9#11   G(add2)   **Chorus**
                                D

_____   Right _____ here, __

D/G

___   right _____ now, _____   I'm

Bm11   G(add2)

look-ing at you,   and my heart __ loves the view, _ 'cause you mean _ ev - 'ry - thing. __

Asus   A   D   3

_____   Right _____ here, __   I prom - ise you

D/G   Bm11

some - how ____   that to - mor-row will wait   for some __

                G(add2)   Asus   A

___ oth - er day __ to be,   and right now ___ there's you __ and me. __
                                        Both:

                                        Verse
D/G   Dsus2/G   Gsus2(add#4)

___   *Female:* If   this were for - ev - er,

                Bm9

what could be bet - ter? We've al - read - y proved _ it works. _____   But in two _

Scream

**Words and Music by
Jamie Houston**

Verse

Voic - es in my head tell me they know best.

Got me on the edge, they're push - in', push - in', they're push - in'.

I know they've got a plan, but the ball's in my hands.

This time it's man to man, I'm driv - in', fight - in' in - side a

love that's up - side down _____ and spin - ning fast - er!

Chorus

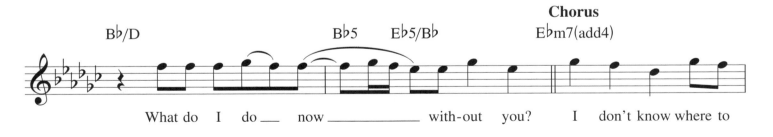

What do I do _ now _____ with-out you? I don't know where to

go. What's the right team? I want my own thing so bad I'm gon - na scream.

40

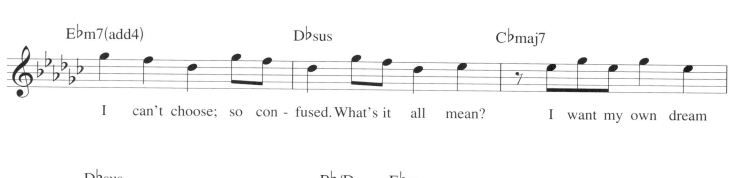

E♭m7(add4)   D♭sus   C♭maj7

I can't choose; so con - fused. What's it all mean?   I want my own dream

D♭sus   B♭/D   E♭m

so bad I'm gon - na scream.

Verse

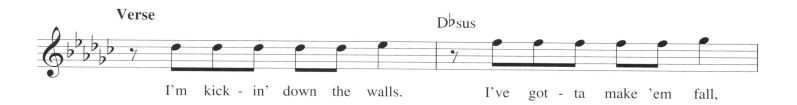

D♭sus

I'm kick - in' down the walls.   I've got - ta make 'em fall,

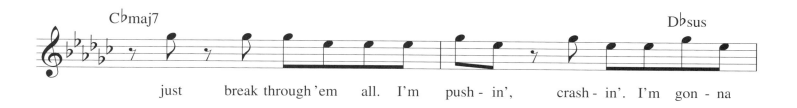

C♭maj7   D♭sus

just break through 'em all. I'm push - in', crash - in'. I'm gon - na

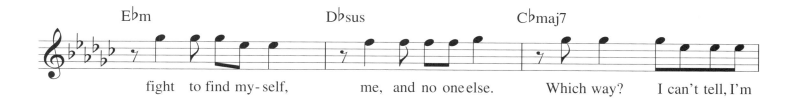

E♭m   D♭sus   C♭maj7

fight to find my - self,   me, and no one else.   Which way? I can't tell, I'm

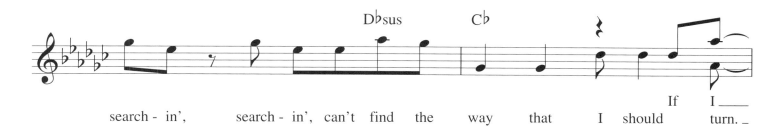

D♭sus   C♭

search - in', search - in', can't find the way that I should turn. If I____ ____ should turn,

D♭   B♭/D

____ should turn, right or left, it's, it's like noth - ing works ____

Instrumental

E♭m7(add4)   E♭m7(add4)/D♭   C♭maj7

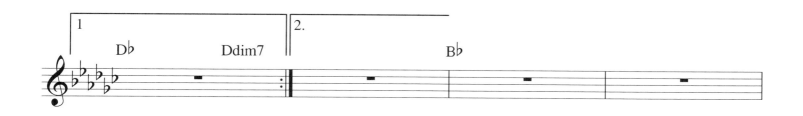

1   D♭   Ddim7   2.   B♭

Chorus

E♭m7(add4)

I don't know where to

D♭sus   C♭maj9   D♭sus   B♭/D

go. What's the right team? I want my own thing so bad I'm gon-na scream.

E♭m7(add4)   D♭(add4)   C♭maj7

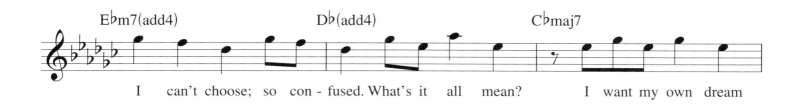

I can't choose; so con-fused. What's it all mean? I want my own dream

Outro

D♭sus   B♭/D   E♭m

so bad I'm gon-na scream.   Ah! ___

Walk Away

**Words and Music by
Jamie Houston**

in' if I stay, _____ oh ___ no. ___ Just walk a - way _

Chorus

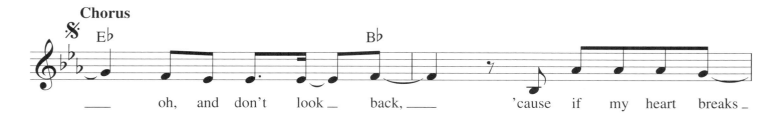

___ oh, and don't look _ back, ____ 'cause if my heart breaks _

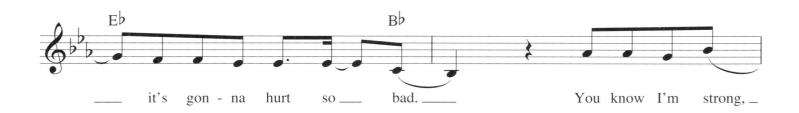

___ it's gon - na hurt so ___ bad. ____ You know I'm strong, _

___ but I can't take _ that ____ Be - fore it's too late, _____

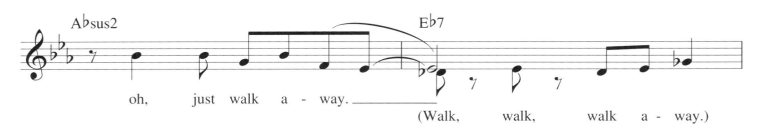

oh, just walk a - way. _____ (Walk, walk, walk a - way.)

To Coda

Ooh, _ just walk a - way. _ (Walk, walk, walk a - way.) _

Verse

I real - ly wish I could blame ____ you, ____ but I know _

that it's no one's fault. _____

Cin - der - el - la with no _____ shoe _____ and a

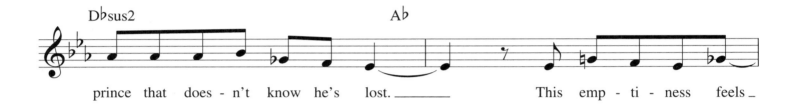
prince that does - n't know he's lost. _____ This emp - ti - ness feels _

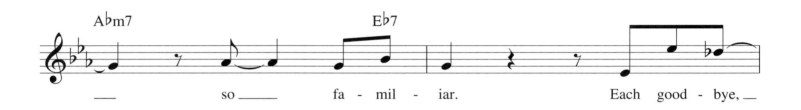
_ so _____ fa - mil - iar. Each good - bye, _

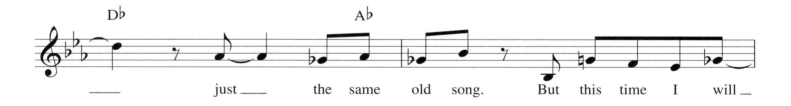
_____ just _____ the same old song. But this time I will _

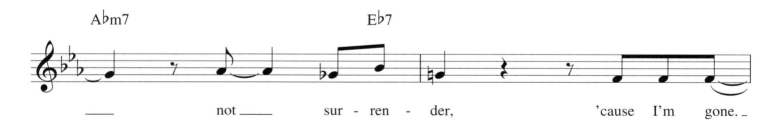
_____ not _____ sur - ren - der, 'cause I'm gone. _

_____ You know I'm gone. _ Just walk a - way _____

Coda

Ab7sus — (Walk, walk, walk a - way.) —

Cbmaj9 — Just walk a - way. ___

Dbmaj9

Cm7 — ___ I've got to let it go, ___ oh, ___

Eb/Db

Cm7 — ___ start pro - tect - ing my heart and soul, ___

Eb/Db

Fm — 'cause I don't think I'll sur - vive ___ a good - bye a - gain, ___

Cm

Db — ___ not a - gain. Just walk a - way, ___

N.C.

F — ___ oh, and don't look ___ back, ___ 'cause if my heart breaks ___

C

F — ___ it's gon - na hurt so ___ bad. ___ You know I'm strong, ___

C

but I can't take _ that ____ Be - fore it's too late, _

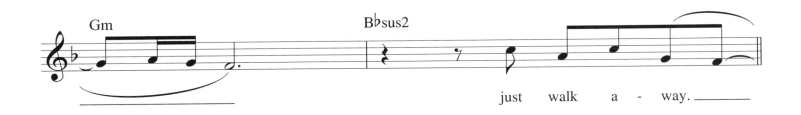
just walk a - way. ____

Outro

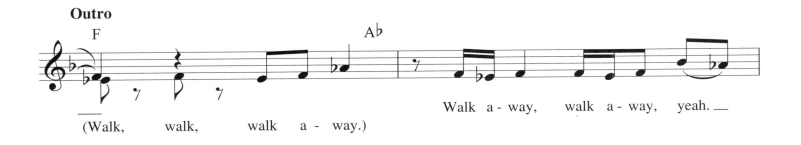
(Walk, walk, walk a - way.)   Walk a - way,   walk a - way,   yeah. _

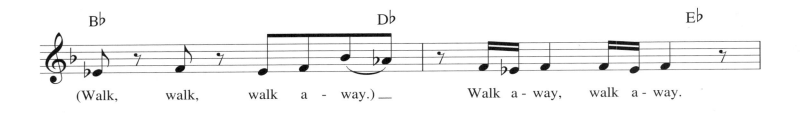
(Walk, walk, walk a - way.) _   Walk a - way,   walk a - way.

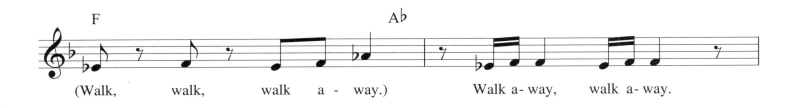
(Walk, walk, walk a - way.)   Walk a - way,   walk a - way.

(Walk, walk, walk a - way.) _   Walk a - way, walk a - way,   oh, _ no.